Tim Burton's
The Nightmare Before Christmas

For information, contact Disney Press, 114 Fifth Avenue, New York, NY 10011-5690.

Printed in the United States of America

10   9   8   7   6   5   4   3   2

First Printing

Characters

Sally

The alluring,
rag-dollish creation
of the evil scientist

Jack

Our hero,
the Pumpkin
King

Oogie Boogie

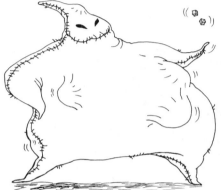

**The meanest
guy in
Halloween
Town**

Dr.
Finkelstein

**The sometimes-
brilliant,
if slightly mad,
town scientist**

Mayor

A political
nightmare

Zero

Jack's ghostly pup

Lock

Shock

Barrel

Halloween Town's
best trick-or-treaters
and Oogie's henchmen

Santa Claus

The jolly old elf
of Christmas
Town

Tim Burton's THE NIGHTMARE BEFORE CHRISTMAS

NEW YORK

He's... finally here!

Boo!

Trick or treat!

Happy Halloween!

Here he comes now.

We're all waiting for Jack!

12

Now for the awards!

Whew.

I hope the doctor doesn't find me here.

Walls fall? You made the very mountains crack, Jack!

Nice work, Bone Daddy.

Yeah, I guess so. Just like last year.

And the year before that, and the year before that.

I know I'm the best there is at what I do.

My name is known all over town.

I can scare the bravest souls.

I've done it forever.

After all, I'm the Pumpkin King!

Jack, I've got the plans for next Halloween.

I need to go over them with you so we can get started.

Jack?! answer me!!!

JACK!

Don't know.

He hasn't been home all night.

Where is he?

ヒュルルル

カチャ

Hmm...

おおおわあ

ああ

あ

Whoa!

くるくる

CHRISTMAS TOWN

Jack, what's happened to you?

Ugh! Smells bitter.

Sally, is that soup ready yet?

Coming!

Frog's breath will overpower any odor.

Lunch!

I want to tell you about Christmas Town.

Mayor,

Thank you.

spotlight please.

わざ
わざ

Listen! Everyone!

グイッ

So, I'll need to show you...

It is too amazing to be described.

Everything was strange and wonderful.

Here in this cell, you'll stay!

Oh, my head!

Up here, my boy!

Jack Skellington!

Come in. The door is open.

Doctor, I need to borrow some equipment.

Jack!

I'm conducting a series of experiments.

Curiosity killed the cat, you know.

Come to the lab and we'll get you fixed up.

Huh?

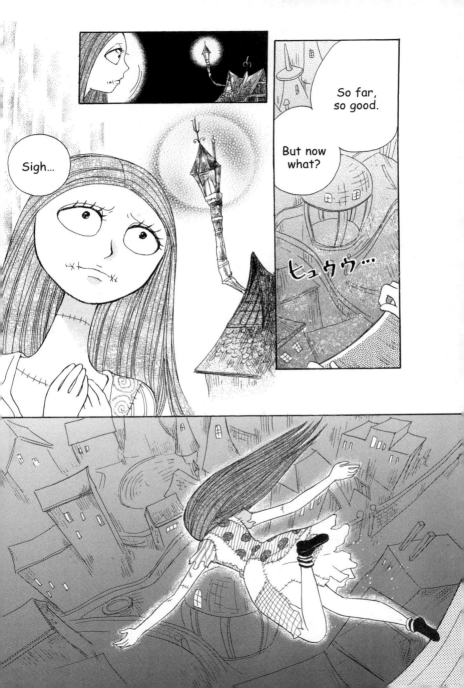

Sally...

I've got to hurry.

...you can come out now...

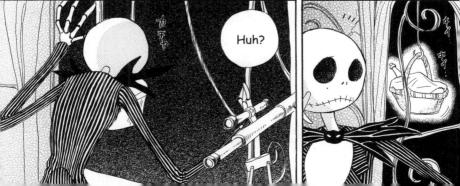

Sally...

はっ

ブルブル

ふふっ

Good
luck,
Jack.

There!

I've got it!

I have my answer.

I was just thinking too hard.

It's been there all the time.

No...

Patience, everyone. Jack has a special job for each of us.

Your Christmas assignment is ready.

Dr. Finkelstein!

Sally!? Grrr...

No problem.

Can it be improved?

What kind of noise is that for a baby to make?

Wah!

We need some of these.

Doctor! Thank you for coming.

Hmm...Their construction should be exceedingly simple, I think.

And do
our job
right.

We
work
for him.

Off
we go.
Ha! Ha!
Ha!

We just make
sure to stay on
his good side.

Now let's
get this
Sandy Claws.

Sandy Claws,
huh?

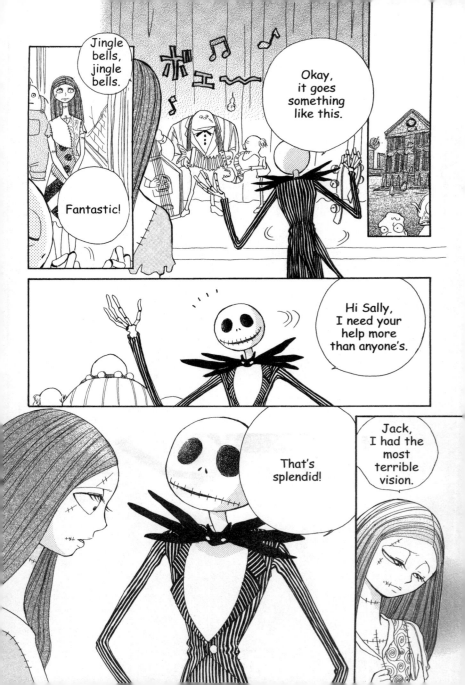

Perfect!

Jack!
We caught
him! We got
him!

Open it up,
quickly!

That's not
Sandy Claws.

HAPPY EASTER

975

You don't look like yourself, Jack. Not at all.

And I feel so much better now.

But you're the Pumpkin King.

Not any-more.

Isn't that wonderful? It couldn't be *more* wonderful!

ハヾキヾ

But...

Jack, I know you think something's missing...

ぶゎっ

うわぁぁぁ

What a pleasure to meet you.

Sandy Claws. In person.

Wh-why, you have hands. You don't have claws at all.

No!

Haven't you heard of peace on earth and goodwill toward men?

...and a chilling New Year!

We wish you a scary Christmas...

This is worse than I thought. Much worse.

No!

Wait, Jack!

Ahhhhhhh!

Merry Christmas!

Strange. That's the second toy complaint we've had.

Hello, police.

Attacked by Christmas toys?

Oh, no...

Santa, wherever you are... come back and save Christmas.

Where's that Sandy Claws?

Jack. Someone has to help Jack...

Whoa. Careful down there. You almost hit us.

They're thanking us for doing such a good job!

Fireworks! They're celebrating!

Sandy Claws was taken to Oogie's place.

Just as I thought...

Are you a gambling man, Sandy?

Ahhhh!

Little Harry and Jordan. Won't they be surprised?

Who's next on my list?

Yow!

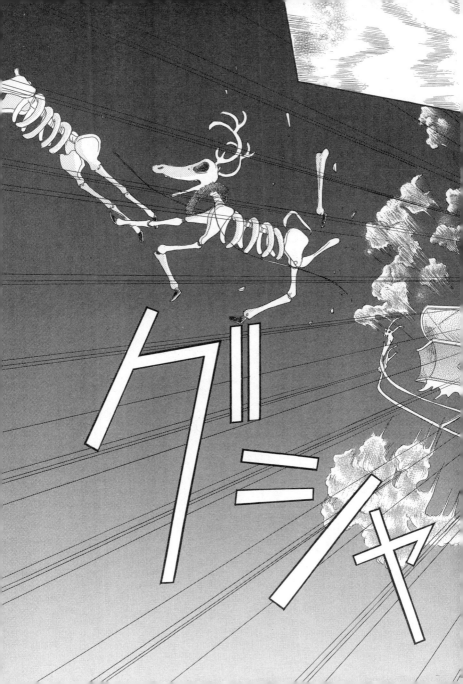

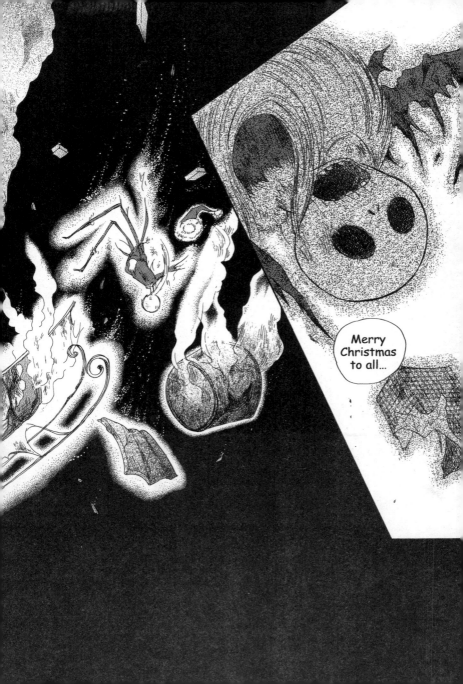

By the time he's through with you, you'll be lucky if you...

You wait till Jack hears about this!

Boogie!

Everyone...

The king of Halloween...

...has been blown to smithereens.

Skeleton Jack is now a pile of dust...

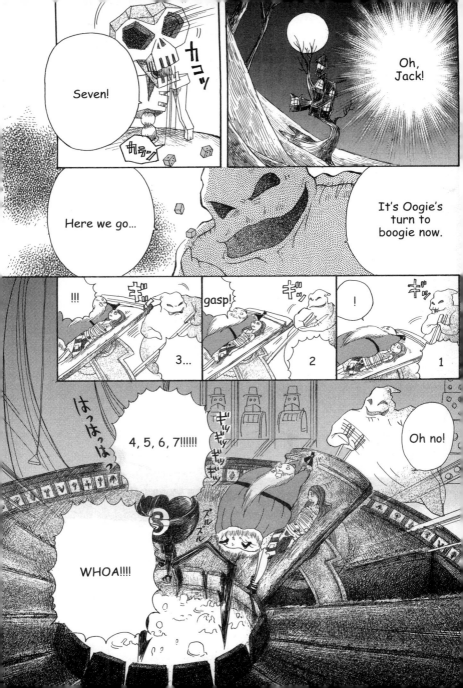

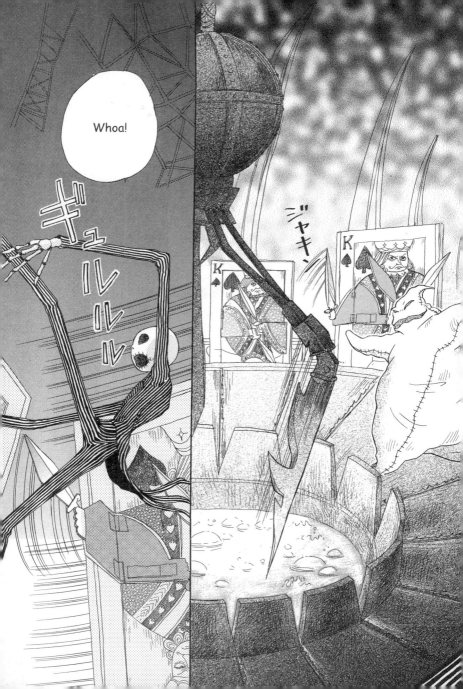

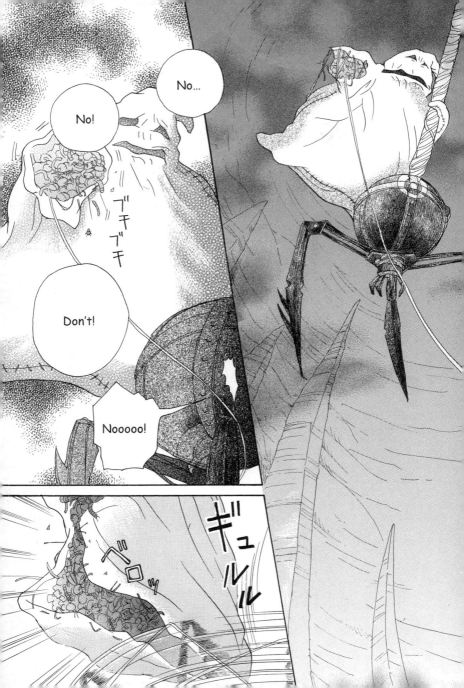

Jack's
back!

He's all
right!

Jack's okay!!

Welcome
home, Jack!

We've
missed
you!

We're glad
to have
you back!

Merry Christmas!

Jack...

The End.

This is...

...the end of the book!

Oops!
You're at the END of the book!

The book in your hands reads back-to-front—the same way it did when it was originally printed in Japan. This not only makes it an authentic experience, but it also allows you to see the art and follow the story just as the writers and artists intended.

Oh, one more thing . . . this book also reads right-to-left! If you're new to manga, here's a handy guide, featuring two pages from the book, to help move you along from panel to panel. . . .

It's simple! Just follow the numbers inside the balloons and get ready to read pure Japanese-style manga!